It's Great to be Kind

Jordan Collins • Stuart Lynch

make
believe
ideas

"Good morning, class!" said the lion with a **roar**.

The children laughed.
They knew it was just
their teacher, Miss Clayton,
in a costume.

"Welcome to Dress-Up Day!"

Miss Clayton said in her regular voice.

"Please take turns telling us about your costumes."

Miss Clayton's
Class

Carly showed off her **dragon** costume.

Emily said, "I like your spiky tail."

"Thanks! I made it myself!"
Carly replied.

Jack spun around so everyone could see his **superhero cape**.

"My dad sewed this from curtains," he said proudly.

"If anybody wants to try it on, they can."

Connor went next. He put a **golden crown** on his head.

"I'm a king!" he said.
"I know all about kings!"

"That's a **fabulous costume**, Connor," said Miss Clayton.

"Thanks," said Connor.

He thought to himself,
I'm going to love being a king –
kings are in charge
of everything!

Soon it was time for reading group.

Connor saw Jack reading a book about wolves.

"I want that book,"

Connor demanded.

"I'm reading it now," said Jack.

"You can read it next."

"Kings don't wait!" Connor yelled, and he grabbed the book.

At lunch, Connor pushed to the **front of the line**.

"That's **not fair!**" said Emily. "Go to the back."

"I can do what I want – **I'm a king!**" said Connor.

He raised his head in the air and ignored his friends.

"I'm a queen, but **I'm not breaking any rules**," Emily said.

"You're **not a queen**," Connor said. "You don't even have **a crown!**"

Emily burst into **tears**.

"It's okay, Emily," Abby said.
"I think your costume is **beautiful** even without a crown."

Then Abby turned to Connor and said,
"You shouldn't make people cry. It's not kind!"
"Kings are allowed to be mean," Connor said.

Still, he felt bad as he watched Emily wiping her eyes.

After lunch, Miss Clayton asked the class to **split into groups** to make finger-paint pictures. Everybody teamed up:

Tia with Sean and Carly,

Ryan with Abby and Sophie,

and Jack with Emily.

Connor was **the only one** without a group.
He felt **sad** and **lonely**.

"Connor, you can work with Jack and Emily," Miss Clayton said.

"Why didn't you pick me?"
Connor asked Jack and Emily.
"I thought we were friends."

"We are friends," Jack said, "but you're **not being very kind** today."
"I'm just doing what a king does," Connor said, frowning.

"Who says kings can't be kind?" Emily said.

"And anyway, you're not a real king."

Connor shrugged.
His face felt hot
and his stomach
was in knots.

Emily and Jack **moved to a different table.**

Connor realized he'd been **unkind** and **bossy** all day.
He'd hurt everyone's feelings
pretending to be a king.

Now he **felt bad** — his friends were upset with him,
and he had **nobody to play with.**
Dress-Up Day just wasn't fun anymore.

Connor walked over to Jack.

"I took the book you were reading," he told Jack.

"That wasn't kind, and I'm sorry."

He handed the book to Jack and said, "Next time I'll wait my turn."

"Thanks!" Jack said.

"You're welcome," said Connor, and he stood a little taller.

Then Connor found Emily.

"I shouldn't have made fun of your costume. I'm sorry," Connor said.

"This is for you." He gave his crown to Emily.

Emily clapped her hands with delight.

"It goes with my costume," she said as she put it on.

"Thank you. You're the **kindest king in the whole world!**"

Even though he wasn't really a king,
Connor felt like royalty when his friends thanked him.
No costume could make Connor feel better than this!

It felt good to be kind.

Now his friends were happy, and so was he.

READING TOGETHER

The Let's Get Along! books have been written for parents, caregivers, and teachers to share with young children who are developing an awareness of their own behavior.

The books are intended to initiate thinking around behavior and empower children to create positive circumstances by managing their actions. Each book can be used to gently promote further discussion around the topic featured.

It's Great to be Kind is designed to help children realize that sometimes their actions can be thoughtless and upset others, whereas acts of kindness make people feel valued and happy. Once you have read the story together, go back and talk about any similar experiences the children might have had with unkindness (and also with kindness). Ensure that children understand that everyone acts unkindly sometimes and that, like Connor, they can take steps to repair relationships that may have been damaged.

As you read

By asking children questions as you read together, you can help them engage more deeply with the story. While it is important not to ask too many questions, you can try a few simple questions, such as:

- What do you think will happen next?

- Why do you think Connor did that?

- What would you do if you were Connor?

- How does Connor make up for being unkind?

Look at the pictures

Talk about the pictures. Are the characters smiling, laughing, frowning, or confused? Do their body positions show how they are feeling? Discuss why the characters might be responding this way. As children build their awareness of how others are reacting to them, they will find it easier to respond in an understanding way.

Questions you can ask after reading

To prompt further exploration of this behavior, you could ask children some of the following questions:

- What can you do to be kind to other people?

- Can you think of a time when someone was unkind to you?
  How did you feel?

- Can you think of a time when someone was kind to you?
  How did you feel then?

- Can you think of a time when you acted unkindly or with kindness?

THE ROSE & THE SHIELD

"With each novel she enchants readers by creating exciting historical settings and the unforgettable romances of characters you come to adore."

CRY OF THE WOLF

"The final release in the Wolf series is as masterful and satisfying as readers could desire. Barbieri pulls out all the stops, drawing together every loose thread in this strong Western, beautiful romance and powerful story about family."

NIGHT OF THE WOLF

"Western sagas are Barbieri's forte and the Wolf series is an excellent example of the memorable characters, broad scope, intrigue, tragedy and triumph that make her sagas memorable."

SIGN OF THE WOLF

"Barbieri captures the essence of a time and place, the spirit of the characters, the jargon, the superstitions and the culture of the Old West. She sets her plot against this colorful backdrop and delivers what her fans most desire: a strong story and the aura of the era."

HAWK'S PRIZE

"A wonderful and satisfying conclusion to the four-book series . . . Barbieri's engaging characters touch your emotions and you get a totally unexpected surprise at the end."

HAWK'S PASSION

"This is an enjoyable read."

MORE *RT BOOK REVIEWS* PRAISE FOR ELAINE BARBIERI!

TEXAS TRIUMPH

"Barbieri brings the Texas Star trilogy to a powerful close, leading readers through a maze of deception, dishonesty, magic, hatred and justice's ultimate triumph."

TEXAS GLORY

"This well-drawn portrait of the Texas frontier, its strong characters and tangled plot twists will keep readers hooked."

TEXAS STAR

"Barbieri gives readers a complex story with subplots, passion, and a love that satisfies from start to end."

HALF-MOON RANCH: RENEGADE MOON

Elaine Barbieri is "a mistress of the complex plot and wild Western. This is the final installment of a not-to-be-missed quartet!"

TO MEET AGAIN

"Elaine Barbieri certainly knows how to capture the reader's attention. Utterly delightful characters, tender romance, and plenty of harrowing adventures make for a splendid Western."

NIGHT RAVEN

"A fast-paced page-turner, *Night Raven* will keep you up all night until you get to the satisfying end."